How do you grieve a loss of a hope you cannot express when you know something is missing?

Thank you to my friends and family for your continued support.

Specific thanks to Dada for your words and KK for your drawings.

Daisy and the Bee: A Story of True Friendship

Once upon a time, there was a bee. He lived in a hive in a town or a place just like yours and mine. It seemed to him that no one wanted to be his friend. All the bees he knew had human friends and he had none. He stayed in the hive as much as he could.

He did not know much as a bee, but what he did know was loneliness. When he did leave the hive, he did not do any of his bee duties. He only searched for a friend. All the other bees in the hive had friends, human friends. No matter what he tried or how hard he tried it, the bee could never make friends with a human.

What the bee did not know was there was a little girl, named Daisy, who also did not have any friends. One day, the girl met the bee. From that day forward, the two of them played and played, until they both had to return home.

A few weeks later, the fun stopped when the bee became

sick, very sick. The bee played one last time with Daisy and

returned to the hive. Daisy never saw him again.

After realizing her friend had died, Daisy become very sad.

She cried and cried until her tears ran out. At their favorite

playing spot, she noticed the bee funeral for her friend.

Daisy joined the ceremony. It was then she noticed how

mad the other bees were, at HER!

What Daisy did not know, what she did not understand, was how all the other bees felt. The other bees realized they had lost one of their own. They were sad and angry at themselves because they were never his friends. Over time the bees began to blame Daisy. They believed she poisoned their friend.

All at once they attacked Daisy. They stung and stung and stung her. Daisy was able to get away. After the stings, she grew very weak. Eventually, she had to be in a wheelchair. Daisy could not go outside because her parents feared that she would be stung again. She became even more lonely and sad.

Daisy's parents were friends with the Mayor of the town.

The Mayor was a proud and protective leader. After

hearing the tragic news of Daisy being stung, he declared a

new law. No human could be friends with a bee.

Before long, more and more people grew to dislike bees.

The Mayor, thinking he was a good leader, hired

professionals to trap the bees and remove their stingers.

"No one will ever be stung again!" The Mayor proclaimed.

The professionals trapped all the bees and put them in a tank. They used gas to make the bees sleepy. Once they were asleep, all their stingers were removed. Later, they were woken up and set free.

The bees were angry that their stingers were removed. They were unhappy they had been changed. They lost all their human friends, and now all their stingers. Because they were so angry at the humans, they decided to stop pollinating all the flowers and plants. It did not take too long before all the flowers, trees, and grass began to die. As the plants disappeared, so did all the town's happiness. Only gloom bloomed.

Eventually there was no color to be seen. The humans all walked out on their balconies, terraces, porches, and front steps. To nothing, to no one, certainly to no bees, they looked around to see everything and saw nothing. They were tired of all the sameness.

With nothing to be seen, families began to move from the town. The first family to move was Daisy's. In a few weeks, all the families had left. The last person in the town was the Mayor. One day, when walking around the deserted town, he found a single flower still growing, pretty and pink. He felt something stir inside himself. Realizing what he had done, he changed the law so that bees and humans could be friends again. He then resigned as Mayor and moved to a new city.

After hearing the law had been changed the bees agreed to pollinate again. As the flowers bloomed, so did Daisy. She could walk again! Daisy's family moved back to the town. Shortly after their return, Daisy's mother was elected Mayor. Her first action was arranging play dates and parties for bees and humans.

Daisy was still sad about losing her friend the bee. While there were other bees, they were not her friend. Then, one day, everything changed. She met a butterfly.

Make friends. Find others that do not have friends and bee their friend. A friend can bee nearby or far away. Bee friends with everyone along the way. Human or bee or butterfly, whether you have a stinger, arms, or wings, none of those things truly matter. What does matter is always being the type of friend that you would want your friend to bee :)

Made in the USA
Columbia, SC
15 August 2024

40121986R00022